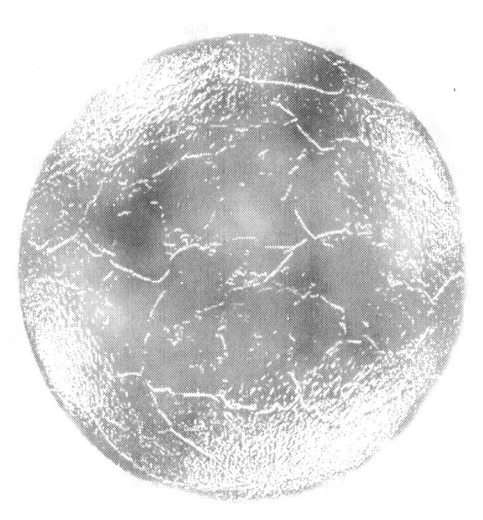

**WITHDRAWN FROM STOCK
AND OFFERED FOR SALE
WITH ALL FAULTS BY
SURREY COUNTY LIBRARY**

Copyright © 2016 Luciain M. Irvine
Cover photo courtesy of Lisa Runnels

FIRST EDITION
Released Monday, October 3rd 2016
Published by Gary R. Smith

Exploits of the Sea
All rights reserved.

http://www.exploitsofthesea.com

ISBN: 1535431849
ISBN-13: 978-1535431842

the
EXPLOITS
of the
SEA

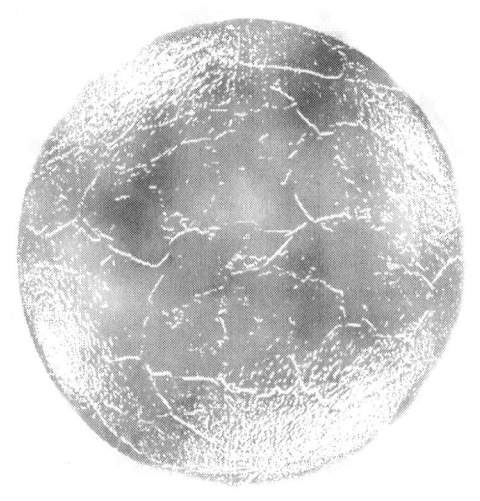

Luciain M. Irvine

Let me be your shepherd,
Let me call you in.
I'll care for you when the foxes pass,
While you graze lovingly upon the grass.

You will always be my special one,
The one shining brighter than the sun.
You somehow take this shameful farm,
And give it a warm, welcoming, loving arm.

Why would you leave me, little lamb?
You've gone away and I have no plan.
Stick with me and before the day is through,
I will have made you ewe.

-The Lamb by Luciain M. Irvine, 2012

Included in this publication

Lucia's Vision

1360 B.C.

THE LAMB

The Fall Trilogy
Volume One: Origins
a preview

LUCIA'S VISION

*A short story written during
National Novel Writing Month*

November 2015

*One paragraph was written per day.
Each was written spontaneously.
It was all published immediately to social media.*

<u>Lucia's Vision</u>

The storm came and the intensity overwhelmed me. I had to ready my vessel. Not only was this my first time at sea, not only were the waves riding higher than my ship but on the horizon, I could see the flashes of mortar shot and the burning of my ally as she slipped under the tide in flames.

I tried to climb over the waves. I could feel the poor girl leaning backwards. I needed to pull her in hard; hard to port.

I could feel her begin to capsize as she marched through the rising wave. My crew worked hard and we held ground. How proud I felt. We steered around the violent sea toward the burning effigy which was once a good ally. Hopefully, we could salvage something, or save a life.

The waves lowered, just enough for me to see the flags flickering on the masts in front of me. From this distance, I couldn't tell if they were friend or foe. It was too dark to tell black from blue in the midnight sky. We stayed our course, but the approaching vessel started firing their guns at us.

Bullets and cannonballs shot past us. I narrowly avoided death and it was all thanks to the roaring waves. I ordered my crew to retaliate, but they were through with taking orders from a woman - let alone one who had never sailed before.

It was a big task for me to undertake. Instead of following my orders, the crew tried to dodge the oncoming attacks and steered us toward the remnants of *Collatine's Heart* burning two hundred metres away.

I had lost control. Swept away from my post at the helm, Carri steered the ship starboard. As the boat turned, cannon fire struck one of the smaller masts, demolishing part of the bow's decking. As the crew panicked and tried to maintain our course, I scrambled into my cabin.

I had to make sure it was still there. As I neared the cabin doors, another cannonball shot into the side of the cabin. Splinters flew far and wide. I was lucky to be alive. I somehow managed to sneak through the doors unscathed as I headed for the lock-away. I hoped it would still be there. To my surprise…it was. The last shard of Thesus still emitting the same green luminance. Now I could get some control back. Now I could regain my power. Now I could reclaim my ship. With the power of the shard in my grasp, *Thesus' Revenge* would be mine again.

This sphere, the last remains of the first breed of pirates, had some amazing qualities. Even though it looked like a metal ball with an eerie green glow, it enabled me to target my foes and bring this battle to an end. Victory at last.

Bringing down *Collatine's Heart*, watching it disappear under the stormy tides, was how I anticipated earning the respect back from a mutinous crew. I plotted the enemy's location on the shard with my fingers and concentrated.

Collatine's Heart was pulled under the Aegean Sea's surface, disappearing without a trace. Far behind us, I could still see the fire-lit smoke above the ship, *Lucrece's*

Dying Soul. Three ships went to battle and only one survived. All that remained was the storm.

As Carri marvelled at the disappearance of *Collatine's Heart*, he failed to notice the rogue wave approaching starboard. I was still in the cabin. I tried to hide the shard before anyone knew how I attacked them. I couldn't let the last shard fall into the wrong hands. The tidal wave struck us hard. Before we knew it we were upside-down.

I dropped it. I felt the shard slip out of reach. Before I could give into my devastation, the water started coming in. I needed to find it again before I ran out of air. I could feel the weight of *Thesus' Revenge* coming down around me. I panicked.

In the darkness, I could see the green shimmer of light as it sank further into the depths. I tried to dive down to retrieve it. The pressure of the water forced its way around my ears and head. In my last attempt, I reached out. It was in my grasp again.

I pulled it in close and tried to kick my way to the surface. Using the shard, I was able to command the weather and Sea-Gods to end this storm, returning my crew and me to safety.

The Gods obeyed my command and, for a moment, everything went dark. Leaving us to drift in the calm sea amongst my broken ship, the Gods spared our lives.

The sun rose as I clung to the debris. It was a beautiful image. I was barely conscious by the time we washed up on the shore. My wet clothes clung to my body as the sun attempted to dry us. I was just able to lift my head enough to see the rest of my crew march toward me along the blazing sand.

My first reaction was to use the spherical shard again, proving my power. I felt around for it before I remembered my last vision witness it disappear in the darkness below the Aegean. Lost forever.

I struggled to know what to do next for fear of what my crew might do to me. They came in closer and Jon pulled me from the ground and bound me to a tree.

The ropes burned my wrists. The crew prepared their weapons to torture and rape me against the scratching bark. I was helpless. Jon came forward, spear in hand. I closed my eyes tight and braced myself against death.

The loud snap of gunfire echoed around us. I watched Jon's body fall to the ground to reveal Carri wielding a smoking musket, defending my honour.

"I saw what you did, Captain Lucia," Carri said to me, holding up his gun to the rebellious crew, "and if any of you *pirates* tries anything else, I have plenty of shots left!"

I was eternally grateful to Carri, but I felt he was stealing my power. I could have saved myself...eventually.

As soon as Carri released me I had to make my exit. What respect did I have now? I should have been able to save myself. I marched away, fumbling in my soaked pockets. As I pulled out the dripping cloth map, I noticed Wenamun's signature still intact. It was still legible. Nearly there now, only a few obstacles left.

I followed the map through the trees and I knew for certain this was the right island. I strolled through the tall palms and double checked my bearings. This path was new. This path was broken.

The map I held detailed a fork in the path ahead, branching into three directions. The crossroads in front of me went off in five. I knew I had to find higher ground so I tried my luck. I chose the fourth path.

I appeared to be heading in the right direction. After following the sandy path for a while, I came to a bridge. It would have led to my destination if the stonework hadn't collapsed.

I peered over the edge. The fall must have been two hundred feet down. As I turned to go back, the rocks under me gave way and I slipped.

As I fell, I could feel the ground support my back. It seemed like a vertical slide. I squealed with delight all the way down until I landed in the wet mud of a stream.

The fog crept in. In front of me, I saw a tunnel entrance in the hill walls. It was dark, but I followed it anyway. I knew it would lead me to Wenamun's shrine. It looked right according to his map. Inside I would find the lost idol of Amun. As I came to the large room, I saw the small statue stare back at me.

I made my move. I needed to gain the idol's power. With the shard lost, I was nothing. This would give me meaning once again. As I neared the statue, my crew found me.

Their mutiny continued. I was thrown into a bloodthirsty battle of swords and wits against them. Twenty versus me. All desperate to steal Amun. As I fought, I clambered over a barrel. Before I knew it, there was an explosion.

I woke at the sound of my village under attack. Was it all a dream, or something more? At the foot of my bed, I saw a parcel left in my name. I never received letters. I was only 7-years-old! Inside, I found a metallic sphere emitting a light green glimmer. The ball sat inside a hemp-cloth map signed by Wenamun.

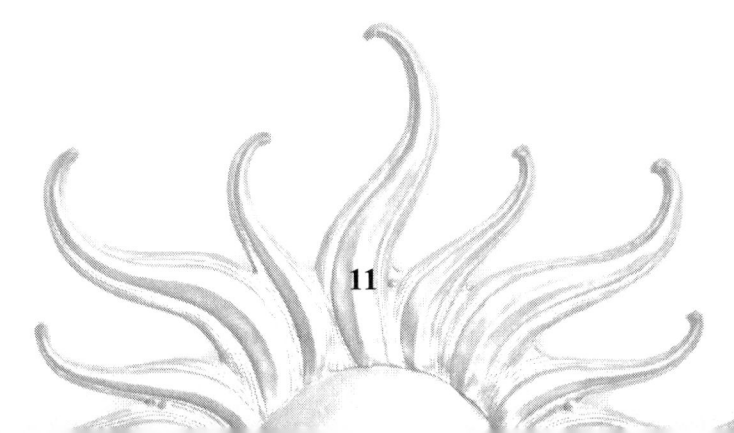

1360 B.C.

A little insight to the time and history surrounding

The Fall Trilogy

1360 B.C.

King Erectheus II had ruled Athens for forty years. The Greek Gods were said to inhabit Mount Olympus several hundred miles north. Civilisation had peaked.

In the heart of the Bronze Age, every city had its ruler, the citizens followed their own laws. Money had not been invented. Payment for goods and services depended on trade. The trade routes crossed the Aegean Seas and reached from Greece to Libya, growing stronger by the day. The world thrived on salt; an essential product with many uses.

The boats and ships were much the same in terms of design, but their size made the difference. All widely spread and shallow, ships were good for carrying an army whereas boats could only carry one man and his cargo.

Peace reigned around the Aegean. Even the most intimate of battles had started to fade.

The written word was still being born. Clay tablets portrayed the basic hieroglyphics, even these were often mistranslated.

The weather was becoming more extreme. Winters were cooling much too fast. Summers were heating intensely. In the centre of the Aegean Sea, the mountain volcano of Thera began to smoke once more.

THE LAMB

*This novella falls between
the prologue and first chapter of*

*The Fall Trilogy
Volume One*
Origins

1	The Temple	1
2	Ambush	5
3	Capture	11
4	Mycenae	17
5	Auction	21
6	The First Night	27
7	The Lamb	31
8	Desire	35
9	Barbarians of Mycenae	39
10	A New Beginning	45

1
The Temple

It was a long, gruelling, ride for Dorian and Collatine. Dorian knew if he was ever hunted down by Melanthius, the city of Argos would protect him and his son. The wind blew through Dorian's flowing hair as he leant into the silver mare. He couldn't help but feel ashamed for leaving his fellow villagers behind but protecting his son was more important.

On the outskirts of the Eleusinian city, Dorian spotted a couple of men in a familiar dress. He slowed Feriou to a quiet pace, trying his best to keep a distance.

"What is it, Dad?" Collatine asked.

"Quiet, boy," Dorian replied, "look at their outfits. They have come from Athens. They are the Royal guards; Melanthius' men. If he is with them, we're in trouble. Stay back, stay hidden. I need to take a closer look."

They galloped through Eleusis, keeping their distance from the Athenian guards, stalking every movement in the Thracian plains. Dorian watched as the guards approached the east slopes. At the summit, Dorian stopped his horse near a thicket of bushes. He instructed his son to stay out of sight with the mare and looked around for a safe path to spy on the Athenian guards.

Dorian had heard stories, but he had never imagined the size and scale of the building. As soon as he saw the pillars leading to the throne room, he knew where he was.

Leaving his son out of sight, Dorian edged his way inside the Temple of Demeter. He kept to the darkened corners, staying out of sight.

"King Eumolpus," the first guard yelled through the echoing hall.

"How dare you enter Demeter's Temple uninvited?" responded a stranger in the shadows, dressed in a dark cloak.

"We were looking for your King," replied the second guard with a timid tone under his voice, "we desperately seek his help."

"I think we have invaded far enough," the first guard whispered to the second in caution as Dorian noticed a few more cloaked men appear in the back of the temple.

"You have indeed," answered

the cloaked stranger, "No-one enters the Mysteries without invitation."

Dorian watched as the cloaked men intimidated the guards, extracting small knives of sharpened bronze inlaid with tin decoration.

"Silence them."

As the cloaked men followed their orders, slaughtering the Athenian guards where they stood, Dorian decided to flee the temple before he was seen.

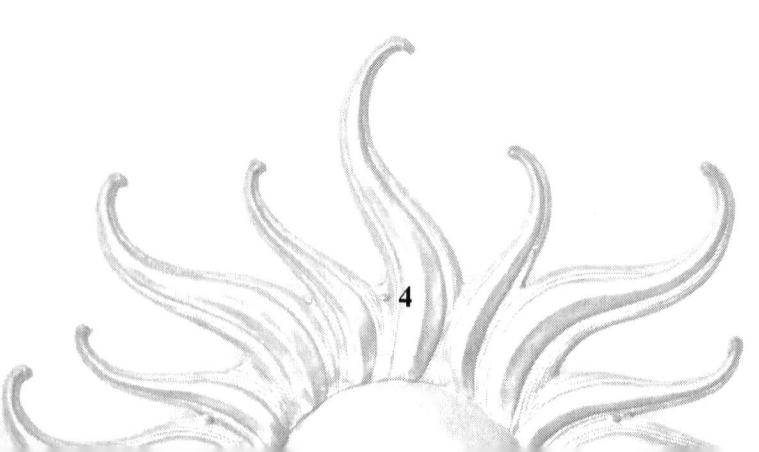

2
__Ambush__

As instructed, Collatine remained in the thicket. He marvelled at the swarming bees collecting the last remnants of pollen in the closing seasons. Dorian rejoined his son and feared what may happen if they were seen by the mysterious cloaked men. Jumping on the silver mare, they rode west to Korinth.

Hugging the shorelines, they kept the island of Aegina in their sight. Each day grew colder than the last. It wasn't long before the bees had vanished for the winter.

After riding through the wide plains, steep hills, and bitter winds they finally approached Korinth. As they stopped to rest before the last day's southerly ride into Argos, Collatine felt dread wash over him.

"Dad..." Collatine whispered.

"I know, son. I can feel it too," Dorian whispered back, slowing Feriou to a light trot, "Easy, girl."

The small valley on the outskirts of Korinth felt unnatural. It was if a hundred eyes preyed on them as they strolled through the open meadow. The trees along the edge formed a passageway for the father and son to conceal themselves. They looked around, no-one was in sight.

The nine-year-old Collatine hugged his father's back tight as Feriou carried them on her back, shielding his eyes from fear. Dorian knew something wasn't right, and felt the urge to kick the mare, making her ride at full speed.

One hundred yards down the

road, an arrow flew out of nowhere and pierced Feriou's neck, sending her to the ground in a cloud of dust.

Collatine was thrown several feet from where the horse fell. Dorian had the weight of the mare pushing down his leg, almost crushing him.

Screaming in agony, Dorian noticed three young men emerge from the trees. They must have only been fourteen but they looked starved and weak. To Dorian's surprise, one of the stick-like boys rolled Feriou off Dorian, dragging her to the side for skinning. The other two took hold of their new captives.

Night fell on the captors and captives. The three scavengers started to prepare a camp whilst Dorian and Collatine watched in bonds. The scavengers had a crude dialect which meant they could only understand each other.

After skinning Feriou, the

youngest man started tearing chunks of raw meat from the bone, piling up the horse meat in steaks on the ground next to the fire. Using the leaves from the trees he attempted to clear the blood from his arms as the meat sizzled over the fire.

Dorian concentrated hard on the boys, watching while they ate. He listened to their hushed conversation, trying to make out what they were saying. Dorian had a way of understanding people, picking up on different dialects and piecing them together. Somehow, Dorian thought it seemed much less fluent than other Aegean languages he had come to know when he spent his youth travelling the waters. The one thing clear to Dorian was the scavengers couldn't share a name among them.

The sweet aroma of crackling horse meat spread through the forest. Dorian and Collatine needed to eat.

They had been starved for too long, and it began to show. The three strangers offered the ripe meats in a moment of compassion. Dorian's hunger was too severe, he tried not to be repulsed by the idea of eating his old pet, but had to give in. Collatine suffered. He couldn't convince himself of being hungry enough. Feriou was more than a horse to Collatine, she was a companion, she was a friend.

Blood rushed back to Dorian's veins as his bonds were cut, allowing the father to bring the hot food to his lips. While the four ate, Dorian took pity on his starving son. The look from Collatine filled Dorian with remorse, and he placed the food on the ground, unable to continue.

Dorian turned his attention back to the strangers. As the scruffy, almost naked, muddy, teens tore at the meats, Dorian realised they weren't savages so much as homeless, fighting for their own survival.

Dorian had proved to the strangers he and his son were no threat. Dorian could have easily fought back to free Collatine and slay the captors, but he chose not to. He let things play out. It began to prove in his favour.

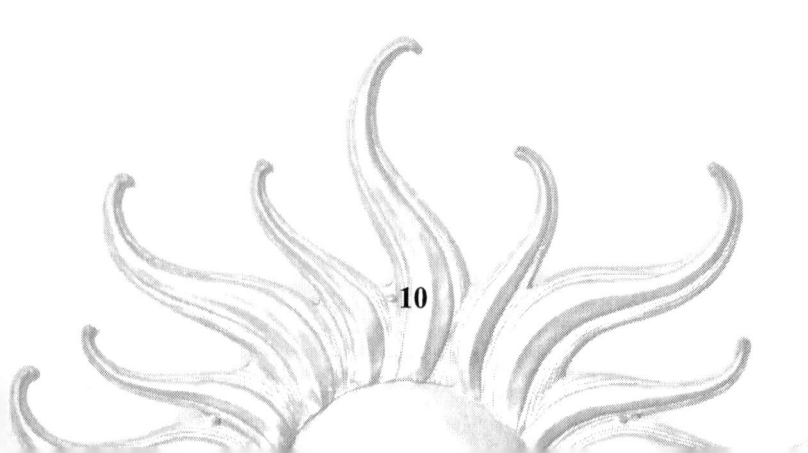

3
Capture

Footsteps pounded their way toward the camp. The smell of freshly warmed meats attracted unwanted attention. By the time a group of hungry barbarians arrived on the scene, there was only one steak remaining. It belonged to Collatine.

The savages panicked, ready to fight for their unit. The invaders outnumbered the scavengers, two-to-one. As the barbaric invaders and the three young savages began to circle, Dorian held back to calm his son.

"Wait here," Dorian instructed, "and don't move. Let me end this fight so I can free you. We will be away soon."

"I can help," Collatine whispered.

"No, my son," spoke the father, "you are too young, it is too dangerous. I need to keep you safe."

As the two groups began to fight, Dorian jumped into action with bare knuckles blazing to help protect the scavengers whom he began to take pity on.

With a swing at the largest of the barbaric group, Dorian punched the brute square in the jaw. Blood rained to the ground from the beastly man's mouth, and instantly the three closest invaders ran to attack Dorian.

Dorian was able to evade the charge, backed by two savages. As he ran away from the on-coming attackers he grabbed a large stick that dangled over the fire. Dorian used the fire-stick to shield himself and the two savages.

"Halt!" shouted one of the remaining barbarians who held the youngest savage in his grasp.

They all turned to the barbarian. He was standing next to one of his comrades who had a mouth full of meat, clutching on to the tied Collatine.

"Why did you attack us?" the brute continued, trying to calm the sudden fight, "We could smell your delicious meats from far away. We were hoping you could share. We have been on the road for days without food. Why did you attack first? We could have dined *with* you."

Dorian tried to speak, if only to say these young men are savages, easily scared and cannot understand the barbarian's native tongue.

"Dare you to speak!" the brute interrupted, assuming Dorian knew the question was rhetorical, "We are hurt. For that, you now must choose.

The boy or prisoner?"

He waited for a response, but Dorian felt confused by the question.

"Boy, or prisoner?" the brute yelled again after a pause, "Which is to die? Boy, or prisoner?"

"The boy," Dorian said without hesitation, knowing the savages wouldn't understand him, "whatever you do, don't hurt my son. I beg of you."

The brute nodded with an evil smirk. He held the young savage high in the air, holding his axe blade to the boy's throat.

The other two scavengers tried to fight to reclaim their brother, but they were held back by the barbarians. Dorian fell to the ground in tears, unprepared for the impending slaughter.

The young boy was thrown to the ground instead of being killed. Dorian breathed a sigh of relief for him but feared for his son. As he watched the barbarian's face change, a sense of evil flooded over the brute.

"No," shouted Dorian as he saw the barbarian swing his axe to the ground, decapitating the scavenger.

Without a chance to comprehend the slaughter, the brute holding Collatine started dragging the prisoner away from the scene. The other savages ran over to their fallen comrade and were too busy mourning the loss than wanting to continue a fight.

The rain started. The death was too much for Dorian, let alone the loss of his son. He tried to run after them, but the lack of energy was too powerful against him. All he could do was scream for his son's return, but the invaders left with Collatine still in ropes; thrown over a shoulder, kicking and screaming.

Luciain M. Irvine

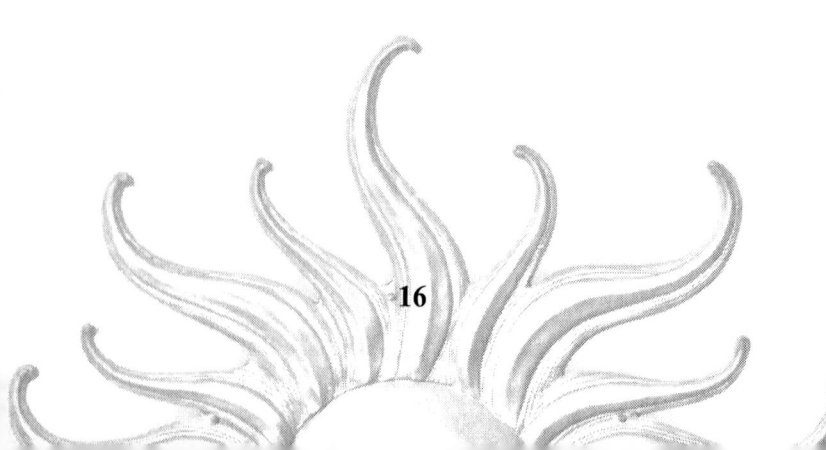

4
Mycenae

Under the cover of a blackened sky, Collatine was carried into a city. The streets felt like a labyrinth; high stone walls and walkways. It was clean. It was cold. It was deserted. Collatine lost all trace of where he was until he was thrown from the shoulder he lay on and hurled into a dank cell.

It was pitch black. He couldn't see past his nose. He could smell the faint juices emulating from a single orange in the corner, muffled by the aroma of festering waste.

For the next three hundred days, this was his life. No light. The excruciating scent pierced his nose and the muffled sounds of footsteps and people talking from above were haunting. The single fruit and the trough of stale river water left for him each day drove him insane.

Alone in the cell, Collatine couldn't stop thinking about when Thesus disappeared. He thought of the sweet five-year-old girl, Lucrece, and her idea of taking a young lamb to play with Thesus, helping to lighten Thesus' mood. The sight of her crying when she saw Thesus being swept away haunted Collatine ever since. The memory of his selfless father still clung to his mind. As desperate as Collatine was to see his father again, he couldn't help thinking all these memories were fading.

He was too weak to move when the light blinded him on the three-hundredth day. A broken heap of nothing, Collatine was dragged out of the cell and thrown to the ground, scraping his arms against the cold stone floor, shaken by the sounds of a cheering crowd. His eyes adjusted to the light. His was not the only body laying on the ground.

Fifteen other young weakened souls, cowering in their rotting clothes, barely able to move. A mix of boys and girls lay huddled in the square. The cheering of the citizens began to quiet as a voice spoke from above the city walls.

Luciain M. Irvine

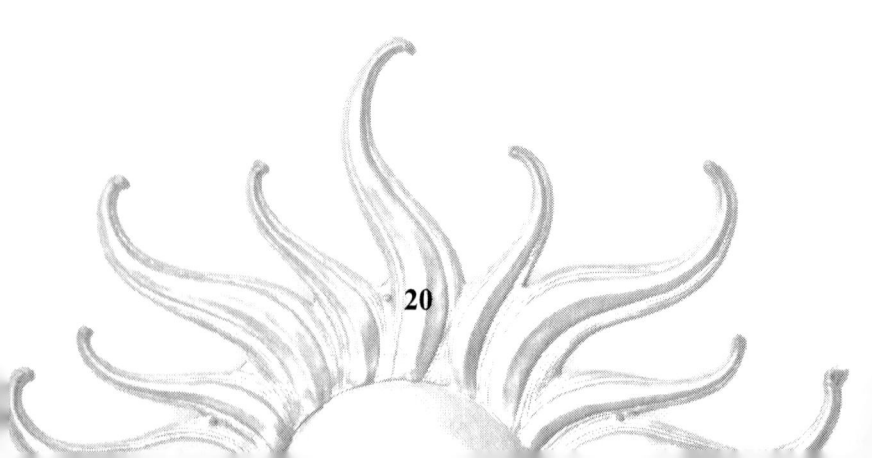

5
Auction

"People of Mycenae; the season has been thrust upon you once again. The browned leaves are beginning to fall and fresh meat has been delivered to help you prepare for the darkening days. There are only sixteen morsels to choose from. Without wasting my precious time, bring me the first."

A guard who stood beside the speaker who grabbed a young girl off the stone floor, tearing her away from the group of huddled children. She was dragged to her feet and placed next to the speaker. He looked her up and down and continued.

"I'd say nine years of age.

Pretty, among the bushy haystack on her head. Feeble arms. Not much now, but a proud wife one day perhaps? I'll start the bidding at three pouches."

People started to contribute their offers. The count continued to rise until she sold for one-half crate. The rest of the children, one by one, were sold off for the best trading offers. Some sold for as little as three small bags. As the children were sold, the bidders diminished, leaving Collatine standing alone with no buyers present.

"Well," said the auctioneer, looking at the lone boy, ready to throw him back in the dungeons, "it seems you're not worth your salt. I hate selling here. I hate to have to throw you back in the dungeon. The people of Argos have it right – if you were treated better, more buyers would want you. This is Mycenae, though, nothing good ever comes out of here."

"Excuse me, Sir," an ageing man said as he entered the square with his young wife, "my name is Eumenes, and this is Korinsia. We don't have much to offer you, I'm afraid, but I will gladly give you this stone carving which I have slaved over for the past two months in exchange for the boy. We desperately need the help."

The auctioneer looked at the stone carving. It was a beautiful finely carved lily with two bees flying around the petals. This carving was a work of genius; one of Eumenes' favourite pieces.

"No salt, no trade," The auctioneer snapped as he held the carving in his grasp, "you know the rules as well as everyone else. The city needs the salt to trade with distant lands and to help preserve our way of life. If you can't give any salt, the boy is tossed back into the dungeons until next season."

Korinsia feared this would happen. She reached into her tunic and pulled out a small leather pouch containing two grammes of salt that she had been scraping together for longer than she could remember. It was a pouch Eumenes didn't know about. The grand sum of their wealth.

"I know it's not much," Korinsia said, "but please accept this. It is all the salt I have, and we are desperate. Take the carving too. Call it a gift, if you will. You could give it to your daughter, she will love it."

The auctioneer looked into Korinsia's saddened eyes and accepted the trade. It meant he didn't have to throw Collatine to the dungeon, and he could put a smile on his daughter's face.

Eumenes and Korinsia were

thrilled to have purchased their slave. It was a long time coming. They had been trying for a child for many moons and had never been successful. The couple took Collatine to where they owned a small dirt home on the edge of the city's stone walls.

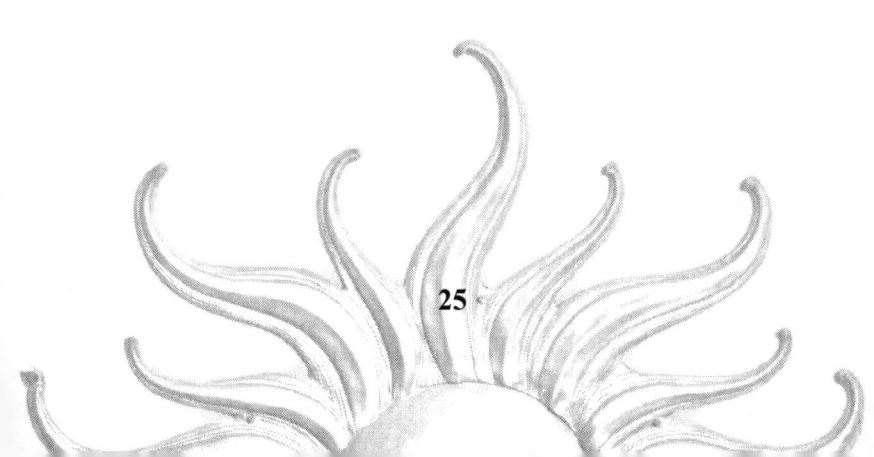

Luciain M. Irvine

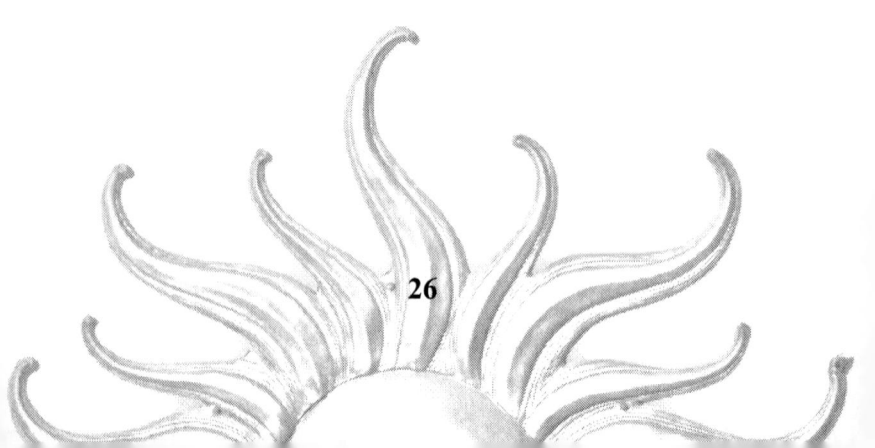

6
The First Night

"Welcome to your new home," Korinsia said to Collatine as they walked into the small, yet spacious, mud-pile hut, "Eumenes, built this home for me from the surrounding earth."

"It's true," spoke Eumenes, noticing the blank expression in Collatine's eyes, "I want you to remember it's your home too."

Collatine stared at the ground, tormented by the dungeons and in fear of his new life, as his new masters as they led him to the main room. Korinsia served Collatine a plate of fresh vegetables with a portion of meat no bigger than his finger.

"We don't have much," Eumenes continued, "but Korinsia is very good with her garden. It's a shame we can't say much about the hunt. As much as I would love to teach you, I can't."

Collatine picked at his food. He was still tormented from the dungeon. His mind wandered back to Thesus. He remembered getting upset when Thesus wouldn't speak to him or his father, but now he understood the trauma.

"I know what you've been through," Korinsia whispered to Collatine while Eumenes went to clean up dinner, "the darkness. The unknown. The eternity. The single piece of fruit left each day. The memories of being locked away in the city crypt still haunts me every night.

I remember my first day on the auction block. The blinding light. The cold stone. The cheering crowds basking in my misery.

I remember being asked my name. It had been so long I had forgotten it. My mind wandered. I knew I was raised in Korinth once upon a time, but my name had vanished from my memory. That's where I came up with Korinsia. I knew nothing more.

You don't know how lucky you are; three times I was sent back into the cells. No-one wanted the girl with one leg."

Korinsia lifted her long brown skirt to reveal a column of wood pressed into the stump of a leg. Collatine had never seen this before. He felt stunned by the revelation and didn't know what to think.

"It was the fourth auction when Eumenes bought me. He treated me well. Before long we married. We've desired a family since, but we've been unable to conceive. Maybe, we could call you son one day?"

Collatine hesitated. He began to feel as though he could speak to Korinsia, but the idea of replacing his lost parents sent him back inside his shell.

As the night fell on the shack, Eumenes and Korinsia showed Collatine to his new room. Wood and stone plates built into the dirt made up a bed and table. Various rags and animal hides kept him warm. As Collatine wrapped up in the warm blankets he couldn't help think of his father.

Hoping Dorian was alive and well, Collatine wished his father was doing everything possible to be reunited once more. Collatine held back the tears for Dorian and concentrated on his vain attempt at sleep.

7
The Lamb

"Time to work," Eumenes shouted, waking Collatine with a rush of freezing, dirty, water thrown over the boy's head, "Get up, now."

Trying to dry himself off, Collatine forced himself out of bed. As he started to dress, he looked out at the early morning crisp.

The sun had not risen over the horizon, but the air was bright and the sky was clear.

Poked and prodded, Collatine was forced outside by his new master while the surrounding homes were awake and the people looked on.

Collatine noticed the masters of

the new slaves leaning against their doors as they watched their new prize tearing food from the ground or scrubbing the stone pathways with splintering sticks to eliminate weeds.

The walk through Mycenae seemed to take forever. Eumenes had turned into a different person in Collatine's mind. He braved what felt like a walk of shame as the Mycenaean people looked on.

Emerging from the other side of the city, Collatine saw an open field with a debris of large white rocks and cracked stones. Collatine was pushed to the largest rock, and as they turned to the other side, chunks were carved from it to make a seat.

"Fetch me two of those stones," Eumenes ordered as he took his place on the rock, "large enough to fit in your hand."

Approaching the pile of cracked stones, Collatine sifted through to find a couple of heavy rocks on the bigger side. Carrying one in each hand, he returned to his master.

"Now we are alone," Eumenes said, changing his tone, "I have to apologise for my attitude today. You have been sold to me as a slave. I long to see you as the son I never had, but appearances must remain. The Mycenaean life is not one for peace, much to my disagreement. It is why I come here. I carved myself this hidden seat long ago, far from the neighbours. If we had a better place to go, I would move, but my legs are too old now, and Korinsia only has one.

I have brought you here so I can teach you my craft. Please, sit."

Eumenes handed Collatine a stone chisel with a fine, deadly sharp, blade. The handle was wrapped in a leather grip, and the silver stone glistened in the sunlight.

"Hold your rock in your palm," Eumenes continued, "and imagine the one thing your heart desires to see it become."

Collatine sat staring into the white stone. It was just a lump. Unappealing. Collatine let his mind take flight for a few moments.

Thoughts of his father and the life they had in Athens. The lone orange in the darkness. The sweet little Lucrece, and the attempt to cheer up Thesus with the lamb. Before his eyes, he could finally see the outlines of a shape appear over the rock in his mind's eye.

"Sheep," Collatine muttered to himself, "a sleeping lamb."

As Collatine looked up to his master. He saw Eumenes smile as they sat together, learning a new trade.

8
Desire

Twenty-one days of chipping away at the stone passed by under Eumenes' instruction. Collatine watched his master cut and scrape at the rock, carefully lining the detail of wool.

Eumenes was a perfectionist. Collatine felt like he spent longer watching Eumenes carve than he spent carving himself. Each tiny detail of Eumenes' lamb was crafted with the greatest amount of care while Collatine's impatience set in and he scraped away at his lamb in half the time.

As Collatine waited for Eumenes to finish ensuring his lamb

was symmetrical, Collatine heard marching and chanting in the distance.

"What is that?" Collatine asked his master.

"Oh, great," Eumenes replied with a sigh, "the mercenaries are home. Barbarians. They're normally running around Greece charged with some task of entertainment or battle for little profit - all in the name of King and Country. It's a wonder why they do it in my opinion. They get no appreciation, just like the rest of us."

Rising from his position, setting the statue and chisel aside, Collatine moved toward the embankment, eager to look on at the approaching horde in the distance.

The barbarians were dressed in animal hides and wearing bronze, skull-shaped, decorative, helmets. Something inside called to Collatine, and he knew he wanted to be a part of their life.

"Maybe they do it for the pride?" Collatine wondered aloud, "Maybe they do it for the love of the sword, a love of the battle, a chance to see the world...or maybe just a way to release their anger?"

Eumenes scorned. Collatine could sense he struck a nerve. On the face of it, this looked like an appealing life, but he was here as a slave. Carving was all well and good for his master but it was not suited for Collatine. He kept the desire to himself, returned to his seat, and carried on carving with Eumenes.

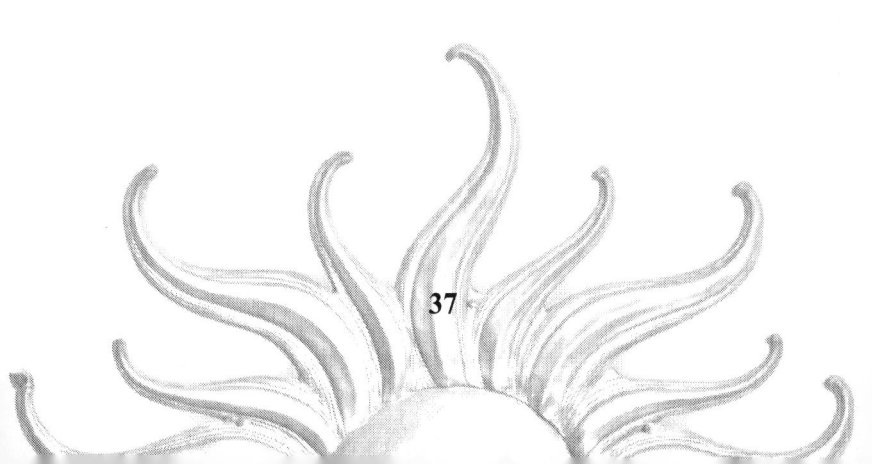

Luciain M. Irvine

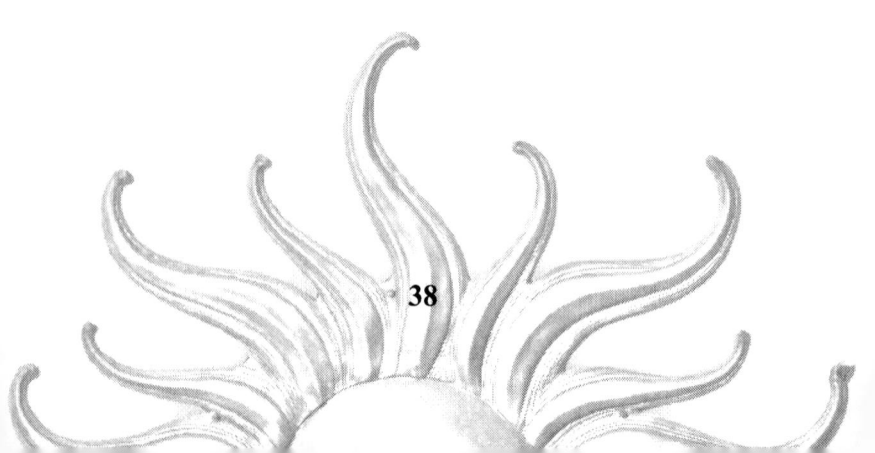

9
Barbarians of Mycenae

Whilst Collatine perfected his talents over the next few years, the growing boy tried talking to some of the mercenaries. He wanted to find out more about their lives and how he could one day become a part of the backbone of the city. None would respond. They didn't care for anyone who was not one of them.

Collatine was getting older. Soon he would be fourteen and he could leave his master's home for good. He had come to love Eumenes and Korinsia as if they were his parents, but he still longed to see Dorian once more. He kept the carving of the stone lamb close to him. It reminded him of his last day in Athens and, with it, his father, Thesus, and Lucrece. It was the first thing he had ever made and every time he looked at it, he could see Lucrece's smile. Even on the hardest of days, it cheered him up.

Cutting away at the grey city walls, Collatine worked on a tablet depicting two royal lions over one of the many city archways. As Collatine tried to keep his balance on the arch, leaning over to carve, he got distracted by the approaching mercenaries. There were only three heading toward him. Without their usual numbers, Collatine hoped one might talk to him.

Lost in his thoughts, Collatine chipped off a small piece of rock from the lion's head. The chipping flew through the air and struck one of the mercenary's skull-shaped helmets with a light tap.

"You ought to be more careful, boy," Boreas said, intimidating Collatine as he jumped from the arch.

"You big dumb brute! You should watch where you're walking!" Collatine said, bracing himself against the monstrous figure of Boreas, "you can see I'm working here!"

The expression on Boreas' face sent a chill through Collatine's spine. The teenage boy almost feared for his life. The stony look from the brute started to turn red as an apparent anger built up inside Boreas.

Collatine stood his ground, poker-faced, and ready for Boreas' retaliation. The barbarian erupted in a fit of laughter. It was as though he could see a younger version of himself in Collatine. It brought an enormous smile on his face.

"Come with me, lad," Boreas

laughed as he barged Collatine through the city, "That's one big mouth you have on you. I like that. Now I want to see how well it controls your liqueur."

Collatine was taken inside a darkened tavern. The room was filled with other mercenaries who seemed to be in competition with their laughter and shouting. He noticed the barmaids trying to fend off the perverted, drunken, men. Boreas called for two jugs of over ripened fruit and vegetable mead as he made their presence known. Collatine felt weak and pathetic in front of the men he admired. He couldn't help but smile.

Collatine felt tested by the men. He started to throw insults back at the group until Boreas introduced the alcohol. Collatine took his first taste. He tried not spit the bitter mead. He tried not to wince as he let the liqueur slide down his throat. He tried not to cough as it burned.

He knew he couldn't show any sign of weakness. It was his key to winning over these brutes.

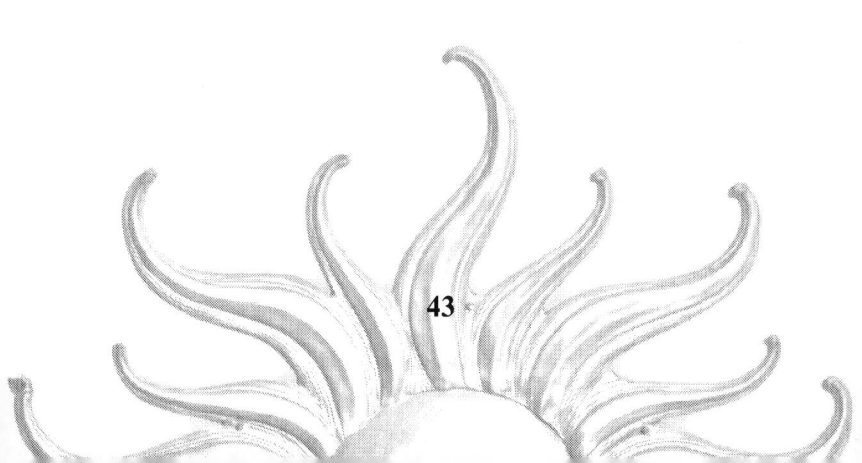

Luciain M. Irvine

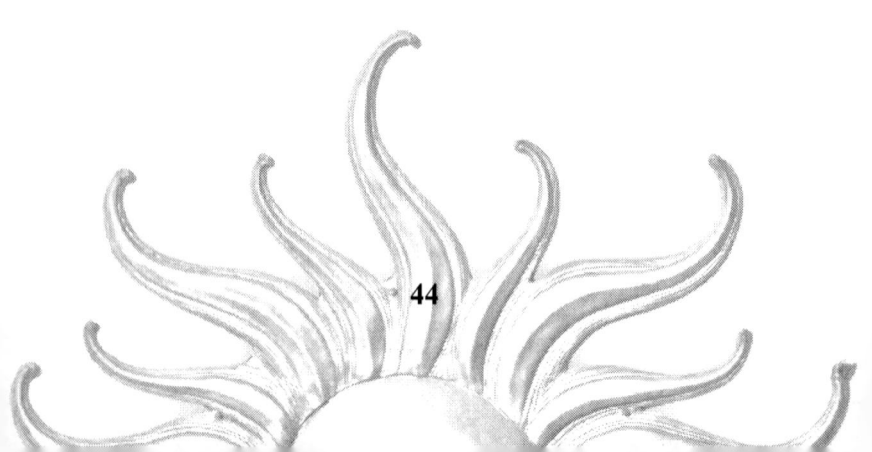

10
A New Beginning

Head pounding and stomach churning, the hung-over Collatine woke in a field. He was surrounded by the mercenaries he admired. Collatine tried to remember the events from the night before but it was a haze. As he sat, he noticed one of the barmaids lying on the ground next to him.

He admired her dazzling red hair. Somehow it reminded him of Lucrece and it made him search his abandoned clothes for the stone lamb.

It was still there. It was still intact. As he stared into it, he thought of Eumenes and Korinsia. They must be worried about him. Collatine had never spent a night apart from them since he was sold. He could only hope they wouldn't be too angry.

"Well, boy," Boreas spoke, standing over Collatine, "you're welcome to join us if you wish?"

Collatine hesitated. The dream of joining the mercenary tribe had come true at last.

He considered his masters. He had to make sure they knew he was safe. He considered the unfinished carvings around the city walls. It was a simple life he wouldn't see again. Looking down at the stone lamb, Collatine thought of his father; maybe they could be reunited if he was to leave Mycenae.

"Let me say goodbye," Collatine asked, "is there time for that?"

"We have to leave now," Boreas said, "We have been called to Eleusis for an audience with Eumolpus. You're either with us or not."

The tribe began their run. Boreas glared through Collatine in anticipation for an answer. As Collatine looked back to Mycenae, Boreas was called by his men.

The teenage boy looked down at the barmaid he had spent the night with. He didn't want to wake her. As he looked back up, he saw the mercenaries had left. With a smile on his face, Collatine ran to them and whispered his goodbyes into the wind.

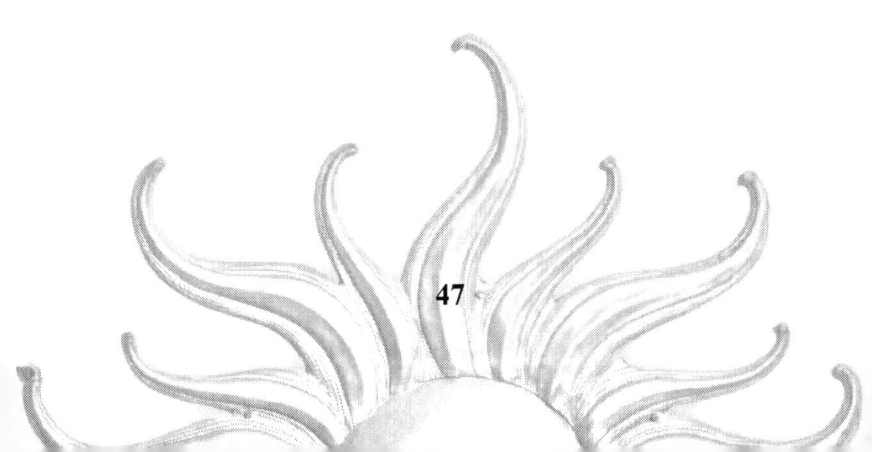

the EXPLOITS of the SEA

The Fall Trilogy

Volume One: Origins

A preview

<u>Knosto</u>

Staring at the ceiling, sleep disturbed, Thesus lay awake; haunted by the memories. Ten winters had passed and summer was arriving once again. Soon it would be morning. Careful not to wake the other slaves, Thesus pulled himself away from his hard, wooden, bunk.

A cool breeze washed over Thesus as it pierced his window. The peaceful stars twinkled in the darkened sky above. As he breathed in the fresh air, Thesus revelled in the calm. It was the best part of his day.

Stepping into the gardens, Thesus looked up to the night sky to see the navy blues edge to a light cyan. The stars began to fade and it reminded him of how the life departed his father's eyes. The stars may have disappeared, but the memory of his parents under the knife of his master remained.

Warming, golden, sun-kissed, colours bathed Thesus as his knees began to ache in the ground; bloody, bruised, and torn by the weeds and crops Lucrece had forgotten to harvest the day before. As the thorns tore at his hands, Thesus couldn't shake the complaint of her sleeping whilst he, once again, did her work.

Lucrece had that talent. She would just flutter her pretty green eyes, flick her wavy maroon coloured hair behind her shoulder, and smile sweetly. Thesus was forever grateful of the pity Lucrece showed him as a child, but could never fancy her. It didn't stop him finding her attractive; he was a man after all.

With Lucrece's work done, Thesus felt he could start his own at last. As the sun warmed, Thesus thought of the tales of golden beaches and hot sands he had heard from travellers who stayed in his home. He could almost smell the salt water. He could almost feel the blazing sand between his toes.

Interrupted by the foul stench of fresh manure as it ejected from one of the horses, Thesus scraped the steaming pile away with his hand. If he washed his foot in the water trough, the horses would get sick, and Melanthius would not be happy.

As Thesus brushed the dirt off from Zeus' smooth body for Melanthius' entrance, there was a sudden crash erupting from inside the stately home. This was not going to be a good day. Leaving Zeus still partly covered in dried mud, Thesus grabbed the vegetable crops and took them inside.

The sounds of scurrying bodies echoed around the brightly decorated halls.

"What's the matter, Emilia?" Thesus asked the crying the slave.

"I knocked over a vase," Emilia answered, "as I walked past Melanthius' room."

"Shit."

Rushing a plate of whatever scraps he could find, tearing signs of mould away from the bread, and pouring brown river water into the master's tankard, Thesus prepared Melanthius' breakfast.

"Take it to him, Emilia," Thesus said, "don't let him get to you, you know what he is like. Make peace. It will be best for all of us."

Breaking the leftovers into twelve equal servings, Thesus felt frustrated at Panos; one of the newer slaves who arrived with Xantes, the slave who should have prepared breakfast for the unpaid staff.

By the time he had placed the breakfast for twelve, Thesus saw a panic of slaves march through the kitchen. Before he could take a breath, Thesus was left with the final dregs of dirt in the water and the last stale loaf covered in a candy floss mould.

"What do you think you're doing?" Shouted Melanthius as he marched past the kitchen doorway and saw Thesus taking a few well-earned minutes, "How dare you sit on your lazy arse eating all day while everyone is running around trying to make sure we are prepared! Don't you know what day it is, slave?"

Thesus looked up in fear at his

master. This was his first mouthful of old bread and breakfast was over. He knew Melanthius was going to be stressed. Not only did his home need to look pristine for the visitors, but the master had also been rudely awoken by Emilia. Without answering, for fear of being answered back, Thesus stood up and threw his breakfast to the scrap bin.

"Why don't you answer?" Melanthius spat as he threw the disobedient, towering, Thesus against a wall.

Thesus didn't know what to say. Whatever he said, it would be wrong. Whatever he did, he would be punished for it. Instead, Thesus took a few deep breaths and prepared himself for the normal punishment.

Eager for seeking the attention of the slaves once again, Melanthius dragged Thesus into the open stables and called for all the other slaves and guards to join them.

Circled by ten house-slaves, Melanthius stood with Thesus on his knees They all knew what was coming; why would today be different? Lucrece stepped forward to present the master with his whip, throwing a look of pity to Thesus. Melanthius raised the brown leather whip, which split off into three plaits, knotted round thick splintering twigs at the tips, and started to strike Thesus on his bare back.

Several large splinters protruded Thesus' bloody shoulder blades. Kneeling in agonising pain, Thesus dared not give Melanthius the pleasure of reaction.

After counting the ninth strike, Thesus took a pause to catch his breath. As his body began to relax, Melanthius dished out one last blow for good measure.

"Now, if I catch anyone else not pulling your weight," Melanthius screamed, "you'll be begging me for the whip. Get back to work, they will be here soon."

As Thesus knelt in pain, trying to pull himself together, he noticed Melanthius throw the whip into Lucrece's arms and storm inside to sit down with a jug of red wine. With the master gone, Lucrece approached Thesus.

Out of the six female slaves, Lucrece wasn't the most attractive, but she was the favourite. She had that glow about her which appealed to everyone. No matter the situation she found herself in, she always seemed to own a cheery, and somewhat cheeky, smile. Thesus always thought it must have been a front considering how she ended up at the mansion, and the things Melanthius had done to her ever since her blood started to come in.

Lucrece placed her arm around Thesus and offered him a comforting smile. Thesus looked into her green eyes and couldn't help but feel his spirits lift slightly. With no more than a glance, Thesus rose from his position and continued to help make Melanthius' home sparkle for the impending charioteers from Olympia, here to celebrate the King's fiftieth summer on the throne.

As Thesus struggled back into the master's home, Xantes pushed past him in the doorway, knocking over the last full urn of water and smashing the clay container against the stone floor.

Unable to contain his anger, Thesus screamed at the young Xantes to collect more water from the river and forced three of the younger girls to pick up the broken shards of clay from the drying pool of water in the morning sun.

Moments later, Melanthius came to discover the cause of the commotion. Thesus' heart began to race. He grimaced at Melanthius' smile he shot to the sight of three young girls on all fours as they collected the broken clay.

"Where the fuck is he going?" Melanthius asked Thesus.

"To the river, Master," Thesus answered with unearned respect, "he dropped the urn so I sent him to get more supplies."

"Alone?" Melanthius roared.

Thesus stood like stone.

"Panos," the master shouted as the young slave passed, "Catch up to Xantes, go with him to collect water. Come straight back."

Panos nodded to his master. Thesus knew Melanthius could trust the slaves in pairs – the fear of

Melanthius' wrath was too intense.

"I told you before," Melanthius shouted, pulling out his blade and sharpening it against a thick leather strap, "I am in charge, or Anetta if I'm not here. You will never be in charge. Now you're really in for it."

As the master prepared to start cutting into Thesus' skin, the sound of the riders from Olympia grew close.

"Melanthius," Lucrece shouted as she ran toward the pair as Melanthius held the blade against Thesus throat, "the riders are here."

"You're lucky this time," the master spat to Thesus, "Lucrece, go and fetch me Zeus. I'll deal with you later, boy."

Melanthius looked over to the stables to see Zeus was still partly dirty. In the hustle of the morning, no-one had remembered to tend to the horses, and Melanthius needed to look his best. He screamed in rage as he could no longer make his grand entrance, and forced the blade into a piece of wood with all his anger.

"New plan," Melanthius said as he began to bind Thesus' wrists with his leather strap, "You're coming with me. Lucrece, follow us to my chamber."

Behind the red curtain in Melanthius' room, there was a wooden hatch embedded in the stone floor. In all his time of being a slave at the mansion, Thesus had never seen, or heard of, the hatch. A long wooden ladder led them through the hidden vertical tunnel that ran through the lower floors of the mansion, and several feet below the ground.

At the bottom, there was a small

corridor which could only just be made out from the light protruding from the trap door high above. They had barely started moving before Thesus' wrists burned in the tight leather.

As the light faded, they came to a large golden bowl enriched with sweet scented oils. An intricate spiral decoration surrounded the edge. The outer rim of the sparkling dish contained a holder for thirteen wooden torches, surrounded the bowl like numbers on the face of a clock.

Melanthius took two torches and dipped the wick ends into the oils. Handing them to Lucrece, Melanthius took flint pieces from his pockets struck them together, allowing the wicks to burn.

With the torches lit, they saw the shelves following the start of the dark passages ahead. They were filled with various treasures. Statuettes of people and animals made out of tin, copper, bronze, stone, and obsidian were scattered among the clay pots laden with heavy decoration.

Lucrece noticed a beautiful statue of a large woman, red in colour, which seemed to illustrate the merging of two great nations in the way her body laid. Thesus was quite taken, though he tried to hide it from the others, with an interesting bronze statue of a man jumping over the top of a bull in an acrobatic style. He also noted to himself the collection of obsidian knives and bronzed swords nearer the golden bowl. As Melanthius pulled Thesus' ropes through the passage, he noticed it.

The snakewood handle. The obsidian. The dried blood stains clinging to the knife. Next to it, a green glimmer radiated off a dull, black ball from which he knew in a previous life.

A torrent of rage built up inside Thesus as he remembered the day he was snatched from the Athenian streets as an orphan and sent to work for his parent's killer. He thought of Melanthius' name for the ball in a discussion he had overheard with the second King Erectheus; it was the *Ferrumstone*. Thesus needed his revenge, he could feel it burning, but he felt powerless against his master.

Just past the shelves, they went through a gate which Melanthius locked behind them. As he locked the gates, Lucrece held her master's torch to the painted walls. Murals of bull-leaping, armies, and bees in the lilies the followed path through the blackened tunnels. The golden skirting along the floor and ceiling glistened in their torchlight.

"What is this place?" Lucrece asked Melanthius in amazement.

"My dear, Lucrece," Melanthius

replied quietly as he gave Thesus a little slack to try keeping the slave-boy out of earshot but failing miserably, "is 'Knosto'. I had this built for myself when I first moved into the mansion, Built in honour of the great King Minos whom I had admired for many years. The rumour of the labyrinth under the palace Cnossus in Crete inspired me. This is how I move around Athens without being noticed."

"Don't you ever get lost down here?" Lucrece asked after they passed the fourth fork in the road, noticing the decorations fade to dirt and every path seeming identical.

"Not at all," The master responded, "remember, it was built for me from my own design."

They kept on moving. Thesus began to wish for his hand to be cut off as the straps felt like they had torn the skin and began working on the muscle beneath.

"Oh shit," Melanthius said abruptly, stopping the trio in the path.

"What is it?" Lucrece said in a panic, thinking for a moment they were lost.

"The parade," Melanthius said, "after the ceremony. I forgot I have to lead it. Lucrece, I need you to go back, get Zeus cleaned up as quickly as you can and take him to the Megaron. I trust you will not let me down."

"But," Lucrece swallowed in fear of the master and what he may do if she doesn't meet his expectations, "how will I find my way out? How will I get through the gate?"

Melanthius handed Lucrece the dull copper key and indicated for her to look to the ground as he knelt. Melanthius showed Lucrece his secret to navigating the tunnels. The golden glint of thread twinkled in the light of the flame.

"Follow this and you will not get lost," He said, "Give me back my key when you get to the Megaron."

She nodded. Picking up the threaded trail, Lucrece and her torch disappeared into the distance.

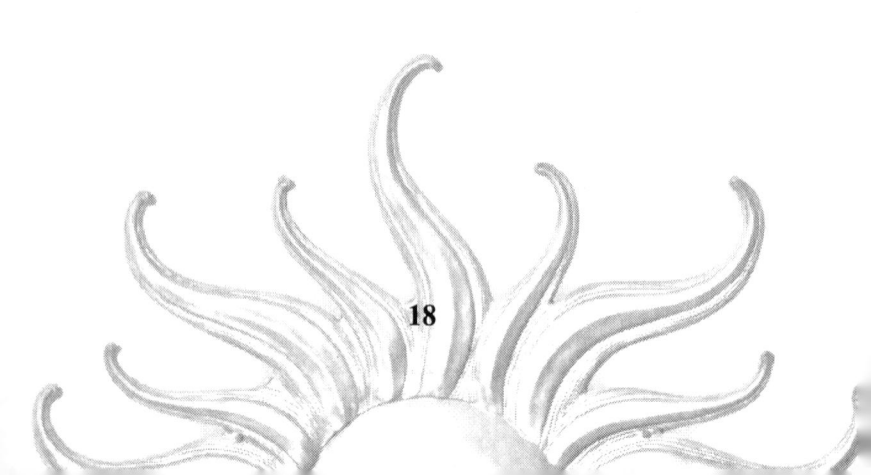

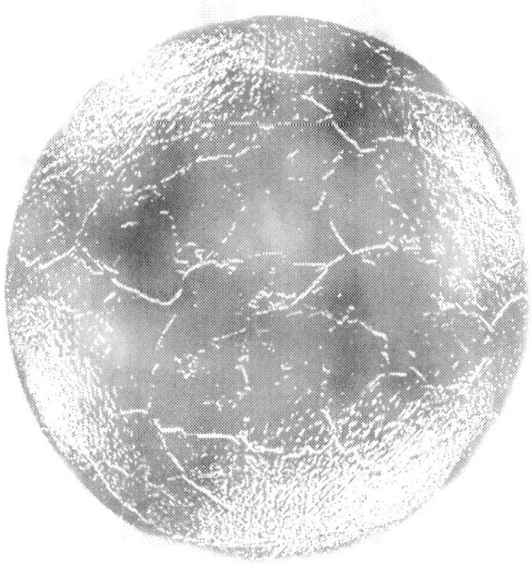

LUCIAIN M. IRIVINE

Writing was never my thing. Music, photography, creating something from nothing, this is what I enjoyed. Family life can be hectic, but when you take those few minutes out to watch a movie with your daughter and a certain question gets asked, ideas spring to life. This is my story.

From this, the smallest spark of a story idea came into my head. With a starting point, I was ready to begin some research. I was not prepared for where it would lead me, nor how long it would take.

Two years went past. The smallest amount of pages written in that time. A tonne of pages filled with ideas and research gathered, I finally had a goal in mind and could see where it was going. With the help of a fellow writer, my first chapter was binned.

Another year later, and four brand new chapters were designed. My writing had improved. I felt like this was doing something at last. Working full time, a house full of children, no time to myself, this was not going to be an easy task going forward.

The powers of social media inspired me to keep going. A total of four years so far, and still sitting on chapter four, the Novel Writing Month was upon me. By the end of the inspiring month, chapter twelve was eventually complete. Only two months later, and the first draft of over sixty thousand words had been secured.

Almost another year later, and still struggling through editing, the decision had been made. I was going to bin another chapter. It was one of my favourites, but the positioning hadn't felt right. The chapter has been revised over, and over, determined to get it right. October 3rd, 2016, over five years after the idea was born, "The Lamb" was released. Helping myself along the way and not relying on other people to do the work for, or with, me, I can call myself an author.

Acknowledgments

Leon for helping me to find my writing voice and guiding me through the process.
Jane for helping with ideas in the earliest stages.
Marianne for being my first fan.
Niko for inspiring Dorian among other ideas.
Dr Salimbetti for guiding me through the historical facts and knowledge of the period.
Tim for encouragement, support, and the little facts that made a big impact.
Claire for advice on finding writing groups and inspiring me to work towards publication.
Freedom for inspiring me to publish this early novella.

Thanks also goes out to all those readers who helped me bring the ideas to life. The readers who have enjoyed and encouraged my work. The readers who have talked about the Exploits of the Sea.

I can't wait to see where this leads to next...

Also Available

The Lamb – Kindle Edition

Includes:-

1360 B.C.

The Lamb

The Scarlet Sunset
prologue to 'The Fall Trilogy: Origins'

Printed in Great Britain
by Amazon